To Baby face
Stay High.!!!

HOW TO ROLL A BLUNT FOR DUMMIES

R.Prince

ISBN:1-59971-758-1

Subversive Publishing

40 Waterside Plaza

New York, NY 10010

Cover Design and Illustrations by

R. Stanton

(512)-294-1073

Book Layout and typesetting: Niwa Kapumbu-Vila

Cover Concept by R. Prince

Contents

1

THE HISTORY OF THE BLUNT

There are many urban legends and myths, concerning the origin of substituting a cigar, for rolling paper to smoke marijuana. Some urban legends suggest that the practice developed in the prison system. Most notably at New York City's famed Rikers Island, were the inmates, after years of growing tired of smoking smuggled weed in toilet paper wrapper and torn pages from the bible, created the method of rolling a blunt. The harshness of inhaling weed rolled in toilet paper wrapper, and bible pages was often hard to take. This is where the term "killing the high", first was used. Also some inmates felt it was sacrilegious, to smoke marijuana, in paper torn from the bible. This might also suggest there was religious implication in the development of rolling blunts. But if this urban myth is true. Then the world must thank that one creative inmate, that first split a cigar down the middle, filled it with weed, rolled it back up, sparked it and birthed the first session using a blunt as the story goes. But there's also another urban myth, concerning a young woman by the name of Candy Williams. A sexy femme fatale, that prayed on old lonely men. Mostly drunk retirees, that were willing to spend the bulk of their social security, or retirement checks for a good time. So on the 1st and 15th of every month, when the checks arrived in the mail, Candy went on the prowl, looking for some old lonely bastard to take advantage of.

As the story goes, one day on the 1st of the month in 1980. Candy Williams went on the prowl, looking for an old geezer that was willing to trick some money. That's when she ran into William Mack, a 68 year old former post office employee, with a pocket full of money to spend for a good time. After a few words were exchanged, both Candy and William agreed to continue their conversation at a local motel, so they could share a bottle of Thunderbird whine and some weed.

Some people swear what transpired next, at the motel, was the beginning of blunt rolling. Only two people know what actually happened. As the folklore goes, William and Candy were butt naked sipping some Thunderbird, about to roll up some weed, when Candy realized they didn't have any rolling paper. Now Candy had to at least get drunk, high, and paid to sleep with these old wrinkled bastards. So she bolted out of the bed, ready to rush to the corner store to purchase some Bamboo rolling paper.

William realizing the value of an erection at his age, had to improvise quickly, to keep young Candy from leaving out the door. He stopped her dead in her tracks, pulled out a cigar, split it down the middle, and rolled up the trey bag of weed, they had just bought. William lit the weed up, and passed it to Candy. The first toke she inhaled, blew her away.

Now Candy being a promiscuous young lady. Would show this new technique of rolling weed, to every guy she slept with. It took just under one year, for Candy to sleep with and show, over two hundred guys how to roll weed in cigars. Some people swear that a freak of the week, is the reason why we all smoke blunts in the present time.

Now before I get off track, because short term memory is hard to come by these days. Let me share with you, the author's memories, of the origin of rolling blunts. I remember in the early 80's, most likely 1984, in Harlem, New York. People, or should I say pot heads, started using white owl cigars to smoke weed in. The first term, or slang for that particular cigar, used in those days was the word "Gotta". I don't know about other hoods across the nation. But back in my old neighborhood, on 127 street and 8 avenue in Harlem, a dilemma arose for us pot heads. Unfortunately, at the same time people started using white owls to smoke weed in. Crack Heads also started using the same cigar to smoke their crack in. Crack heads preferred this cigar, because the white owl possesses a slow burn. This enabled crack heads to steam on their crack longer.

The terminology for their weed, and crack mixture, was known as a "Woola". In the early days of the crack epidemic, sometimes one, would call a crack head, a "Woola-Head" or "Woo-Head". Now this new development in the hood, created a unique dilemma for us pot heads. If you were caught buying a white owl cigar, you were suspected of smoking crack. So pot heads, around my way, switched from the white owl cigar, to the Phillie Blunt cigar. This is were the term, "Philly" but most notably the term, and slang "Blunt" arose from. And the rest, as they say, was history.

During the early 80's, two things happened to the hood that would change things forever. The first was the crack epidemic, and the second was the introduction of the blunt. Rolling paper quickly became obsolete. Pot heads in the hood said good bye, to Easy Wider and Bamboo, and said hello to the Phillie Blunt. During the early years, of smoking blunts, no one outside the hood realized what was going on. Store merchants just thought young kids enjoyed smoking cigars all day. The police didn't know what was going on, and neither did White America.

In the early days, smoking weed in a blunt was just a guilty pleasure most pot heads in the ghetto enjoyed on a regular basics. But after a couple of years, the cops caught on to our little secret. They most likely discovered about it, by interrupting a session, of some young brothers smoking out in some hallway in a housing project. The pioneers of smoking and rolling blunts, came from the projects of New York City. So it would only be a matter of time, before the cops would put two and two together.

But there was one singular event, in pop culture that promoted smoking weed in a blunt to the masses. That singular event, was the creation of rap music. Towards the late 80's and early 90's, rap artists, started rhyming about smoking weed in blunts. Since 70 to 80 percent of people that buy rap music, are white kids from the suburbs, smoking weed in blunts went from being a secret in the ghettos of New York City, to becoming the standard norm for smoking marijuana in America.

These days everyone from the President of the United States, to the skinny Librarian at your local public school, knows what smoking a blunt means. And smoking blunts now crosses, all social, and economic barriers. You would be surprised, at who smokes weed in blunts these days. Its not just the group of young black men, walking down the street. Or that young white kid, with his pants sagging, and baseball cap twisted backwards. It's lawyers, doctors, accountants, just about everyone smokes blunts these days.

Cigar companies are also keenly aware, their product is being used to smoke weed in. Strawberry and vanilla flavors cigars are now marketed to the consumer. These cigars are only being produced for a specific market. That market being us the pot heads. In short, the history of the blunt, has become something much more then most people would of ever imagined. And that's becoming a part of American history itself.

2

MARIJUANA VARIATIONS

There are various strains of marijuana. The number exceeds the scope of this book, however we generalized, and narrowed down the strains into four categories...

DIRT WEED

This strain of weed should be considered the step-child of marijuana. The THC count is very low, and the texture of the weed is dry, stem and seed infested, and all around a horrible high. After smoking dirt weed, many pot heads complain of severe headaches. If at all possible, try to stay away from this strain of weed.

CHOCOLATE WEED

This is a reliable and consistent strain of marijuana. It has a sticky, and moist, texture with minimal stems and seeds. The high various from good, to great, but you will usually, never be disappointed when lighting up chocolate weed.

chocolate weed

HYDROPONICS

HAZE

This is the cream of the crop of marijuana. It's grown under water in a tank, and is referred to as hydroponic marijuana. This strain of weed, has extremely low amount of seeds and stems. The potency of this weed is very high, and will have you stone out of your mind at times. Some pot heads are afraid to smoke it but all will admit Haze is that raw!!!

SOUR DIESEL & CUSH

Two potent exotic strains, which is also expensive. The Cush variation is a much stronger strain then sour diesel.

HOME GROWN

We must give an honorable mention to home grown weed. Since we're discussing the topic of marijuana variations. During my lifetime, I've encountered home grown weed twice. The first time was during the early 80's, when I first started puffing out. Me and my fellow pot heads, were going through a drought. We were all dead broke, and couldn't

Haze

afford a nickel or trey bag to light up. Things were looking real dim. That's until, a member of the crew, showed up with some home grown weed, that his uncle had given him.

We quickly went up to my house to light up. Once we rolled the home grown weed, it wouldn't light up or burn. It was too fresh and hadn't dried out yet. We took the home grown weed, and stuck it inside of the oven for five minutes, to dry it out. Our quick thinking method worked and we lit up. The weed didn't get us too high, but at least I could say I smoked out on home grown. Something that every true pot head should be able to say.

My second encounter with home grown weed happened during the late 90's, when I paid a visit to my brethren, so we could start a session. Once inside his house, out the corner of my eye, I saw six huge marijuana plants, at least five feet tall growing in one of the bedrooms. I almost passed out, it was one of the most beautiful things I've ever seen. I approached the plants staring at them in awe. Its an image, that I will take with me to my grave.

At that moment I wanted to be friends with my brethren for life. I figured if I stayed close to him, I could smoke for free, the rest of my life. Unfortunately, two weeks later something happened and all the plants died before they could be harvest. After the plants died, I cut off my friendship with my brethren. I figured what's the use of being friends with a fucking idiot, that let six weed plants die under his care. I shed a tear till this day for those poor plants that didn't get a chance to grow up and get smoked.

If you ever decide to try your hand at growing weed you should pick up a copy of 'High Times' magazine. The bible of smoking weed. You should be able to find all the info you need to start home growing your weed. And with today's prices, I'm not surprised more pot heads, ain't trying to home grow their own supply. The only thing I know about home growing weed, it's the female plant that gets you high. So if you grow the weed, make sure its the female, not the male plant that you're trying to grow.

3

BLUNT VARIATIONS

Here's a break down of the cigars:

PHILLIES BLUNT

This cigar is the name sake, for the term "Blunt". The Phillie is a reliable cigar that doesn't burn too slow or too fast. But if the cigar is rolled the wrong way, the Phillie can burn up very fast fucking up a session. The taste of the cigar is minimal and goes into the lungs very light.

WHITE OWL CIGAR

The stigma of smoking a White Owl and smoking crack has long been gone. However, the white owl cigar is a very harsh cigar to puff out on. If rolled the right way, the cigar can burn for a very long time prolonging a session. The taste is heavy and it's rough going down the lungs, but its slow burning capabilities, makes up for all its other short comings.

DUTCH MASTER

Smoking Dutch Master cigars took off in the early 90's. It's a good cigar, it has a long burn and light taste however if you don't pack it full with weed it can take on a harsh quality. It's also hard to roll sometimes because the second layer of cigar paper is unstable and falls apart. You must have skills or "Tech" to properly roll a Dutch.

ROLLING PAPER

We must pay homage to the godfather of rolling weed, and that's rolling paper. Most of us old school blunt smokers, either started off with Bambu or Easy Wider. In general most rolling papers are too harsh, but there is an exception, there's an outstanding rolling paper manufactured in Spain, which goes under the brand name, King Size Smoking Green. What makes this rolling paper unique, its made entirely from Hemp paper. It has a slow burn and there's no harshness when inhaling. Since the paper is made out of hemp, its like smoking nothing but pure cannabis. The only draw back, is a pack of this rolling paper, runs about four dollars at some stores. But its well worth the extra cost.

4

THE SCIENCE OF SMOKING A BLUNT

BREAKING DOWN THE WEED

Prior to cracking the Blunt it is advisable to break down the weed. Breaking down the weed consist of removing seeds and stems from the marijuana. Seeds are very dangerous, because they can explode and pop once fire comes into contact with them. Stems can also put holes in the blunts, preventing it from burning correctly. You should always break down the weed on a flat and clear surface. Books, CD's, and DVD's, make good surfaces to break down the weed on.

***The author also recommend that you use this book to break down your weed on. You can flip the book to its back cover and there is a spot designated for breaking down your weed.

It should take between 2-10 minutes to break your weed down. Any thing under two minutes, will not sufficiently disperse all of the seeds and stems. We can not implore to you the great importance of removing seeds from your weed. A near fatal accident occurred in Compton California two years ago. LaShawnda Jenkins age 23, was in such a haste

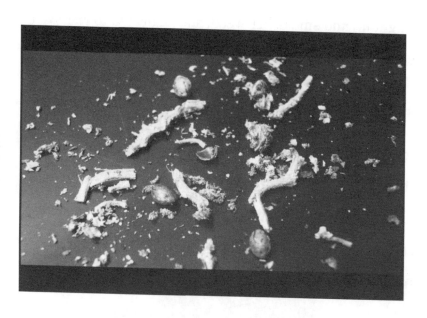

to light up and smoke her weed, she neglected to remove the seeds from her weed, before she roll it up.

It was estimated anywhere between fifteen to twenty seeds were packed inside her blunt. Mid way through the blunt, while watching 106 and park on BET, the blunt exploded. This surprised the hell out of LaShawnda, but what made matters worst was LaShawnda just had her hair done by her cousin, which met there were flammable chemicals in her hair.

The explosion from the Blunt ignited her hair and soon her entire head was a ball of fire. LaShawnda was lucky enough to survive the accident, but 80 percent of her hair will never grow back again. And now LaShawnda must walk the earth with the unenviable title, of being a "bald headed bitch", all because she was too lazy to break down her weed. Let that be a lesson for you. Break down your weed thoroughly.

WEED CRUSHER

This is one of the greatest invention for pot heads since the invention of the bong. Surprisingly, only a few people know about this handy tool, for breaking down weed. Weed crushers come in two forms, which happen to be wood or plastic. Its a circular device which can be broken into two parts.

Once the device is separated, place the unbroken down weed on one part of the weed crusher. Then by returning the device to its original configuration, and turning the crusher in a counter clockwise direction several times, the weed becomes broken down ready to smoke within seconds. Any blunt head that uses a weed crusher, even once, will fall in love with the device forever.

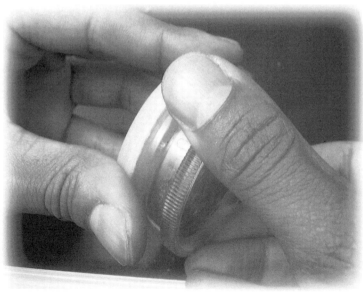

SPLITTING THE BLUNT

Some say splitting the blunt is an art in itself. Great care should be applied when splitting the cigar down the middle. The incision on the cigar must be a straight line. A perfect split can produce a perfectly rolled blunt. That's if the roller is experienced. If the split is not completely straight, in some rare cases this can affect the burn on the blunt in a negative way.

RAZOR

For amateurs it is recommended that you use a sharp instrument, such as a knife or razor. The split begins at the tip of the blunt. Cut gently at the top, then drag the razor back, cutting a straight line all the way down to the base of the cigar. You must have a steady hand when splitting the blunt with a razor. This will insure that the slice won't be crooked.

Once completed, turn the cigar upside down, so the split is facing the floor or the ground. Let the tobacco, or "blunt paper", fall into a waiting bag or garbage. It's advisable, to wet the blunt immediately with one's saliva, before the air dries up the blunt, making it harder to roll.

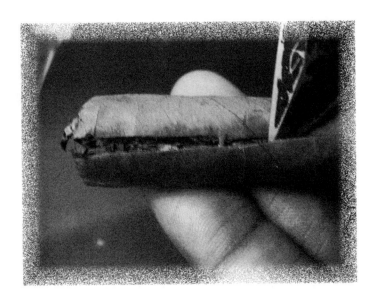

FINGERS

There's a more advance technique to cracking the blunt. Only pros can properly commence with this, and that's cracking a blunt with your fingers. When you observe someone in a session cracking a blunt with their fingers, this person should be given respect. Because he has put in years of paying dues, when it comes to participating in sessions.

To crack a cigar with your fingers you must do the following. First, you grip the cigar with two hands, but only use the thumb and the index finger on each hand. Once you have a firm grip on the cigar, use both thumbs to press down on the tip of the cigar, creating a small but straight break in the cigar paper. Once the break has been created use your thumbs and in a steady motion continue pressing down on the cigar, and the small split you created earlier will grow bigger. Its your job to guide the split, all the way down to the base of the cigar. This is done with a steady but firm application of pressure on the cigar. Empty the guts of the blunt into the trash and begin your roll.

ROLLING

Once the weed is broken down and the blunt is split in half. Its time to roll up. It's advisable, to moist the cigar, with one's saliva, before rolling up. Using your thumb and index finger, from both hands, you will create the matrix roll. The matrix roll is the first roll, which will determine if your roll, will be difficult or easy.

Once the first roll is completed. It will usually take up to, three to four rolls, or twist, to successfully roll a Blunt. The most important twist is the last one. We call this one the tuck. The tuck will determine if the Blunt has a slow burn or will burn up too fast. The object of the tuck, is to roll it tight. However, not so tight that it restricts air flow inside the blunt.

Once you completed the tuck, the best way to see if you have successfully created a slow burning blunt, is to put the blunt to your lips and inhale. If you feel air moving through the blunt unrestricted, then you have succeeded. However, if you inhale on the blunt and feel a restricted air way, it is a high probability, the Blunt won't burn correctly. In this case, the term "The blunt won't pull", should be applied. The best thing to do, is try to re-roll the blunt before it dries.

rolling

SAVING A DUTCH MASTER

There's one cigar that must be mention separately, (if we're discussing the art of rolling a blunt) and that cigar would be the Dutch Master. Its one of the most trickiest cigars to roll. Since its also one of the most popular cigars to roll up with, special attention must be given, when it comes to saving a Dutch Master. Most times when rolling a Dutch Master, the top layer of cigar paper, that consist of three sheets will disengage from the bottom layer.

Once the top layer disengages, it breaks off, into three separate pieces. Sometimes rolling a dutch, can be one big headache. Now most people make the mistake of trying to continue rolling the blunt once the top layer disengages. It becomes very frustrating, and clumsy trying to reattach three different pieces of top layer, back to a split cigar. What's a pot head to do, when all eyes in the session are on you, and you're fucking up the blunt.

First thing to do is don't panic. Second thing to do is not to try and roll the blunt the usual way. To save the Dutch, do the following. First thing is to take the top layer and put it to the side. Take the bottom layer and spread the weed evenly, make sure all seeds and stems are gone. Now you can proceed to roll the Dutch Master with the bottom layer only. Be gentle because the single layer of cigar paper is very delicate and thin. Once you roll the bottom layer completely, take the top layer and wrap it around the bottom layer which will create a perfectly roll dutch.

INHALING

The former Commander in Chief, Bill Clinton, was just an ambitious candidate running for the Presidency of the United States, when he came out the cannabis closet, and confessed to his fellow Americans, that he had smoked his share of potent weed in his lifetime.

When confronted with allegations of marijuana use, the savvy Bill Clinton admitted to smoking weed but claimed he didn't inhale. Now pot heads across the nation, read between the lines, deciphering Clinton's cryptic statement and we realized, not only did Bill smoke weed in the past. He probably had an ounce of Columbian gold, in his pants pocket, while he was answering the reporter's questions.

You see next to rolling a blunt the most important aspect of getting high is inhaling the weed. The first time most people smoke a blunt, they don't actually inhale. Inhaling weed for the first time isn't easy. So when President Clinton claimed to reporters that he had indeed smoked weed but didn't inhale, his answer was so plausible, only a seasoned pot head could give such a believable answer.

Now inhaling weed isn't easy. Before you attempt smoking a blunt for the first time, one should practice inhaling. Just like when you're seeing your doctor, and he tells you to breath in, and breath out. Just do that a couple of times and you'll have inhaling weed down pack. One must remember, (most times) the first time you think you're inhaling, you're not really inhaling into your lungs. You're inhaling and holding the weed in your throat. When you inhale deeply into your lungs you'll know it, the cough that will follow, will shake your lungs, cause your eyes to turn red and tear slightly. And once that intense cough happens for the first time, you'll know you have truly arrived.

5

THE SESSION

The term session refers to a group of pot heads smoking marijuana in a cigar. A session can only happen if two people are engaging in puffing out. The number should never exceed more then five people in the session. If there's more then five people in a session, the term "Too many heads in a session", is often used. And the term "Head", refers to someone participating in a session.

It's also preferred that every head that's participating in the session has contributed the adequate amount of money for the session to take place. Two dollars is the lowest one can contribute to a session without getting cursed out.

Only a selective few heads can join a session without putting in any money. These heads are usually people that have donated before or have sparked or started sessions with their own weed previously. Usually females will get a free pass for obvious reasons. However, if the said female is a chicken head, loud and obnoxious, or wearing lip stick, the bird doesn't get a taste of the blunt. However, the lip stick rule can be ignored if the said female is really cute or has a banging body.

TOKE RATIOS

When participating in a session the most important etiquette to follow is "not to steam the blunt". Therefore one must follow toke ratios when engaged in a session. A "toke" refers to a single, inhalation of marijuana, from the blunt. Another suitable term for toke, is the term "pull". From our research and close to twenty years of personal experience of engaging in sessions, the following ratios should be applied when taking a toke from a blunt.

TWO PERSON SESSION

When two heads are engaging in a session there's more flexibility when it comes to taking a toke. On average, each head can take up to five tokes easily.

THREE PERSON SESSION

Once the session reaches three heads the number of tokes drops by one and the maximum amount of pulls should never exceed five.

FOUR PERSON SESSION

At four heads in the session, the number of tokes drops once again, and should not exceed more then three tokes per head. Once a session reaches five heads, we must then move on from toke ratios, to blunt ratios. One blunt is not enough to get five heads high. Therefore more blunts must be added to the session.

BLUNT RATIOS

One blunt can get four heads high if each head sticks to the allotted three tokes. However, it is very hard to get a good high from one blunt, once you have four heads in a session. More weed must be introduced to the session. That means more Blunts must be lit up. The following are blunt ratios for sessions over five heads.

FIVE IN SESSION

There must be two blunts simultaneously burning for the blunts to rotate three times.

SIX IN SESSION

It will take three blunts burning simultaneously to reach the three rotation goal. As each additional head joins the session, a blunt must be added to the cipher.

BLUNT VIOLATIONS

HOLDING THE BLUNT TOO LONG

There are those among us, with the unusual behavior of holding the blunt too goddamn long. This behavior always fucks up a session. Their greedy, morbid, behavior is something that shouldn't be tolerated. Doing so will only fuck up the flow of a session.

Since blunt holding is such a major and wide spread problem amongst blunt smokers. We decided to interview MARION FORD, age 32, the only man we know in the country, (or the world for that matter) that has sought out psychiatric help for his chronic blunt holding. Mr. Ford gives us a glimpse into the psyche of a chronic blunt holder.

So Mr. Ford when did the transition occur when you went from just another guy in the session, to the despised blunt holder?

It probably started the first time I ever smoked weed.

How old were you the first time you started smoking?

I had to be around thirteen or fourteen years old. Back then we weren't smoking blunts we were smoking weed in Easy Wider paper. So technically I was a joint holder before I was a blunt holder.

Here's the question that everyone in the world wants to know. What makes you hold on to the blunt? Isn't it obvious you should pass it in a timely matter?

At first I thought I was just suffering from some sought of OCD (Obsessive Compulsion disorder). It wasn't until I sat down with a psychiatrist that I realize what my problem was.

What made you go see a Psychiatrist for your problem? Not too many pot smokers would go see a shrink for that type of problem.

Well a good old fashion ass whipping is what prompted me

to go seek help. I caught a real serious beat down, by some fellows I barely knew while I was smoking out in a session in Brooklyn. It was the second time I had stalled out and held the blunt for over two minutes. Those Brooklyn cats didn't ask me the second time to pass. They just started to beat my ass until they left me laying in the street with two black eyes and a couple of broken ribs. When I was in the hospital laying on my back, feeling sorry for myself, I decided to get help for my problem before holding the blunt too long gets me killed.

DID THE PSYCHIATRIST DIAGNOSED YOUR PROBLEM?

The doctor I saw helped cure me of my problem. From what he told me my subconscious mind is trying to steal the blunt. Subconsciously, by holding the blunt, I'm hoping that other people in the session will forget that I have the blunt. That way I could run off with the weed and smoke it all for myself.

SO BASICALLY YOU'RE SAYING BLUNT HOLDING IS JUST A SYMPTOM OF BEING A GREEDY BASTARD?

That's one way of putting it.

Marion Ford's candid comments about being a blunt holder, can help blunt smokers world wide understand what they are up against. From Mr. Ford's own story there's one way to help correct blunt holding. When you catch someone holding the blunt too long, beat the shit out of them. It seems to work in some cases. But there's another violation much worst then blunt holding and that's the...

BLUNT PREDATORS

What's a blunt predator? Its that bastard that never chips in any money for a session. But has his/her greedy ass their waiting to get smoked out for free. These individuals make a life long careers out of being a blunt predator. Some predators are better then others but like the old saying goes, "God don't like ugly", and god definitely don't like blunt predators.

There's a famous story about a notorious blunt predator by the name of Otis Johnson. By all accounts Otis was a despicable bastard, always broke, forever borrowing money. Yet his claim to fame was his uncanny ability to be at the right place at the right time. Some old school blunt heads from Otis's neighborhood boast that Otis had "blunt raped" over three thousand sessions before he turned twelve years of age. By the time his twenty first birthday arrived, every weed smoker in his neighborhood hated his guts.

But one day his luck ran out and things turned ugly for our blunt deviant. Fed up with Otis greedy predatory behavior, some thug out, weed heads decided to exact vengeance on Mr. Johnson. Jason "Vorhee" Williams, and Ted "Bundy" Porter, were so feared they got their nicknames from a real life serial killer, and the lead character from the Friday the 13 film franchise. Most people around the neighborhood were intimidated by these brutish men and stayed clear away from them. Everyone except for Otis. So desperate to get high for free, Otis would often "blunt rape" these two dangerous men's sessions.

There was no denying, Otis was playing with fire. Frustrated, every time he lit up a blunt, a human vulture would appear out of nowhere. Jason "Vorhee" came up with an ingenious plan. Using close to fifteen, 9mm bullets, Jason meticulously broke open the casing and extracted the gun powder from the ammunition. Jason proceeded to create an exploding blunt. By packing some potent haze weed in the front of the blunt, and placing a haze bud in the back, this camouflage the smell of gun powder which was pack to capacity in the middle of the blunt.

Jason being such a criminal genius created a blunt-weapon. Which would carry felony charges, in at least fifty states.

So on Christmas day 2004 at approximately 5:15 PM. Otis Johnson spotted Jason "Vorhee" Williams and Ted "Bundy" Porter engaging in a session on a local park bench. Otis had already "blunt raped" four sessions earlier that day. He was already high, however his scavenger instincts took over. He headed over to "blunt rape" yet another session.

Jason and Ted were delighted to see Otis appear on the scene. Otis quickly made himself comfortable on the park bench and Jason without hesitation pulled out the exploding blunt, lit it up, and quickly passed it off to Otis. That's when Jason and Ted excused themselves from the session. Jason nonchalantly told Otis he could puff out and keep the blunt he was smoking for self. Otis was somewhat emotional hearing the good news. Little did he know he was smoking the Hiroshima of haze blunts.

Once he was all alone with his prize possession. Otis started steaming on the blunt. It took him no time to reach the center of the blunt and the gunpowder. Jason and Ted were hiding far off waiting for the explosion to happen. Their wish soon came true when they heard the loud boom. And saw the bright flash of light coming from the exploding blunt. Shocked by the ferociousness of the explosion Jason and Ted took off running, not wanting to be implicated in what just had occurred on the park bench.

As for Otis? Once he regain consciousness he found himself resting comfortably, in an intensive care unit, of a local hospital. He soon learnt the explosion had given him whiplash. Blew out five of his front teeth. He was also missing half of his nose. Soon after that people in Johnson's neighborhood heard about his misfortune. They started to joke, Otis was suffering from N.D.S,. Which stood for Nose

Deficiency Syndrome. Right now Otis is going through rehabilitation in Los Angeles. Working with a plastic surgeon that has done extensive work on Michael Jackson.

FEMALE BLUNT PREDATORS

There are many ironies in life and one of them are the female blunt predators. These pretty, dick teasers, will smoke up all your weed and your chances of getting some ass is slim, to none. What can you do about these trifling, greedy hoes? Hell bent, on smoking up all your goddamn weed. Actually nothing. Why pass up the chance to spend some time with a honey. Sure she's smoking up all your weed but hey, if you smoke shorty out with some potent weed, and you play your cards right, you might get some ass. I said slim to none. I didn't say impossible. Let's just face it fellas, we're suckers for the females. And let's keep it real. Any man that spends the majority of his time with other men might be suspect. Break away from your fellas every now and then and support you local female blunt predator. They need love too.

HOW TO KEEP A BLUNT PREDATOR OUT OF YOUR SESSION.

THE RE-LICK AND PUFF

Just about every blunt head hates to watch the licking process. Which unfortunately happens to be an essential part of rolling a blunt. Its just something very unnerving about watching someone else lick, then cover with saliva, something you're later gonna stick into your own mouth. This fact can be used as psychological warfare against the blunt predator. By over licking the blunt and saturating it with saliva, you have a good chance of turning away most blunt predators. But be warned. There's a rare breed of blunt predators, that wouldn't care if the blunt fell into a pile of fresh dog shit. So this mild tactic won't deter hard core blunt predators.

"I GOT A COLD".

No one likes to catch a cold or get sick. So by pretending to have the flu or a bad cold you can scare away a lot of blunt predators. However, one must be a good actor to pull this off. Coughing, sneezing, runny nose, and lethargic movement, is the trademark symptoms of a bad cold. Remember these simple facts and execute your acting job as if you were Robert DeNiro preparing for a role.

FAKE COLD SORES.

By placing a drop of ketchup on your lip and letting it dry for five minutes, will give the appearance you have a cold sore. This works 99% of the time.

THE STALL OUT.

There's nothing worst for a blunt predator then staring at an unopened bag of weed. Accompanied by a unwrapped blunt, sitting right in front of him. This will drive him crazy. If one stalls out and refuses to roll up for at least, an half an hour, most predators will get discourage and leave.

MISDEMEANOR BLUNT VIOLATIONS

"NO TECH"

The term "no tech" refers to a person that doesn't possess any technique, when it comes to rolling a blunt. This person should never be assigned the task of rolling the blunt. Because this individual will fuck up 9 out of 10 times when it comes to rolling up. It can be described as a travesty when this person attempts to roll a blunt. Most times they will roll it too tight so it doesn't pull correctly. Or the blunt is unrecognizable after the roll is complete. This person should definitely be kept away from a Dutchmaster cigar. The paper of that particular cigar doesn't stay attached once its split open and this cigar can cause major problems for a person with "no tech".

TOO MUCH SALIVA

Every now and then, you come across someone you smoke out with, that always puts too much salvia on the tip of the blunt. It seems these individuals always possess too much salvia on their lips, or try to tongue kiss the blunt once its passed to them. Now this is a major violation, because no one wants a blunt passed to them with someone else's salvia all over the tip. Once this violation is committed it should be quickly pointed out. If the violation happens a second time in the same session this person should be expelled from the session immediately.

HAVING A COLD

There was a rumor a few years ago, the Center for Disease control in Atlanta, were debating if they should distribute a warning that sharing a blunt with someone with a cold could help spread the flu. Whether this rumor was true or not. One should always be on guard for someone with a cold trying to sneak into a session.

HONORABLE MENTION

THE DEALER

We must give an honorable mention to all the dealers out there in America (and beyond). Without them there would be no sessions at all. If it wasn't for that Dread, with the raw chocolate. Or the Dominican Papis, with Haze and Cush, life would be miserable for the average pot head. There's three type of dealers, that every pot head must deal with from time to time.

THE SUPREME CLIENTELE

This dealer keeps the unnatural raw weed. Its so strong and potent that it scares you when you smoke it. You don't get much product when you spend with this dealer. What you miss in quantity you make up for in potency. You must treat this dealer like family.

THE CONSISTENT RAW

This is the dealer you buy from every day. His product is good and will get you high. However its never potent and won't get you stoned out of your mind. Since the high is real predictable you know you're spending your money well. You must also treat this dealer like family. But only on occasion.

THE GARBAGE MAN

This dealer fucks up the game. He sells garbage weed, catching you on occasion, when you can't find your regular dealer, or you're traveling in a different area. The weed he sells is garbage and will give you a headache. Avoid this lame cat at all cost.

THE WEED SPOT

We can't mention the word dealer, without mentioning the spot. Now the weed spot has many manifestations. To simplify the term, the best and most simple way to describe the weed spot, is the place you get your weed from. What does a weed spot look like? Any person or persons, selling weed at a location, whether indoor or outdoor qualifies to be a weed spot. Some weed spots are outside of buildings, in alleyways, on strips or somewhere in the trap. While other weed spots are grocery stores, candy stores, record stores, clothing stores or any other store that can sell merchandise as cover.

Pot heads can spot a weed spot from a mile away. Most civilians can't tell the difference between a legitimate establishment and a house of cannabis. But us blunt heads have a special type of radar that always leads us to the right spot. Here's some tips that might help you locate a weed spot near you.

1. If you see a ice cream store with a big, tall, Rasta with dreads selling ice cream behind the counter. That's a weed spot.

2. If you enter a Bodega and all the food products are old and stale but they have a fresh supply of dutch masters and Phillies. You're in a weed spot.

3. If there's a small clothing store that stays open to 12 at night everyday, including Sundays. That's a weed spot.

4. If there's a candy store that small children never frequent. And all the regular customers range in a age from 17 to 55. That's a weed spot.

Now don't take my generalizations to heart. Not every example will be correct. It takes a keen eye and experience, to pick out the weed spots that surround us daily. But be rest assured, if there's weed being sold, there will be dedicated pot heads out there supporting their local weed spot.

6

THE SYNDROMES

PARANOID AND LOVING IT!

Marijuana is a hell of a drug. It's been said to cure the sick, inspire artist, and make retarded people less talkative. But the major down side to weed, is that it makes you paranoid. After years of smoking weed, I've realized that I'm not addicted to weed. I'm addicted to the paranoia. Of course being paranoid is not a good sensation but it does make you feel alive. When you're paranoid, adrenaline is running through your system, your mind is working on over load and your senses are heighten.

So I've come to realize, I might be more addicted to being paranoid, then the weed itself. Focus is important in dealing with weed induced paranoia. When focused you keep the paranoia in check. You remind yourself that you are high. Without focus a blunt head can be a bit out of control. They can feel that they're being challenge more than usual. It is not wise to walk the streets in this state. You will feel that all eyes are on you.

PHANTOM SOUNDS

Often times when one is high, he will encounter phantom sounds. These are sounds you swear you heard but once you investigate, there where no sounds after all. Some of the sounds you might hear are the following

Somebody get the phone.....

RINGING PHONE

This often occurs when you are high out of your mind, and you're watching TV, or listening to music. You'll swear you heard the phone ringing. When you go to check, there's no phone ringing, it's just good old paranoia.

DOOR BELL

This too happens a lot when you're watching TV or listening to music. You'll hear the door bell or someone knocking on the door but after further inspection you find out that you were just hearing things.

Who's callin' me?

SOMEONE CALLING YOUR NAME

This is the strangest one of all. And usually happens when you're outside all by yourself. After smoking some weed, many times you'll swear you heard someone calling your name. When you turn around to look, the only person standing there is paranoia.

Are people staring at me???

ARE PEOPLE STARING AT ME?

Sometimes when you're high you'll think people are staring at you. In actuality people might be. But one reason they are, is because you're staring at them. Thinking, that, they're staring at you. So instead of worrying if people are staring at you, just think of it as a plus. The reason people are staring at you is because they think you're great.

DO PEOPLE THINK I'M HIGH RIGHT NOW?

Often time pot heads will smoke weed then engage in social activity. During this interaction the pot head will constantly worry that people think you're high. You know what? In most cases, they do know you're high. But not because you're acting high, or that your eyes are red. Its because weed odor sticks to your clothes. If you know someone that smokes cigarettes and you give them a hug or in close proximity, you can smell the odor of cigarettes. Well guess what buddy? Your clothes smell like weed all the time too. Stop using Visine. What's the good to have clear eyes, when your clothes smell like weed.

TALES FROM THE PARANOID

Warren "Peanut" Robinson one day suffered a bout of weed induced paranoia so intense the incident changed his life forever. During the hot and humid days of summer time, in New York City. Warren would meticulously iron his "White Tee" shirts until perfection. Most people would easily tire at the mundane task of ironing clothes. But Warren loved turning an ordinary wrinkle tee short into a crispy "White Tee".

Another reason Warren loved to iron his clothing was

because he would roll up, and smoke a blunt while doing so. Warren believed that smoking weed turned ironing clothing into an art form. But there was a flip side to Warren's little guilty pleasure. Every time he stepped out the house, decked out in his ghetto fabulous (and well ironed) attire. Still high from his solo session, he would suddenly suffer a slight panic attack. Worried if he turned off the iron, before he left out the house. If he didn't turn off the iron. There would be a good chance, he could burn down his house.

The paranoia induced from the weed would make his mind race in a thousand directions. No matter what he was doing. If he was at work, hanging out, or on a date. He would hurry home to make sure he unplugged the iron.

Fed up with his paranoia. One day Warren decided to fight the urge to run home and check if the iron was unplugged. It dawned on him, the only reason he was running home to check, if he unplugged the iron, was because he was high. The weed was making him paranoid. It took him a minute to overcome the urge to rush home to check but after fifteen minutes of paranoia hell, the feeling soon disappeared. Warren was able to enjoy the day without being a slave to the feeling of paranoia. When Warren returned home he was devastated to see that his apartment had burned down. Later the fire Marshall would tell Warren that he forgot to unplug the iron inside his apartment before he left out.

Moral of this story? If you're just starting out as a pot head, or you're already a seasoned pro, with years under your belt. We all suffer from the same paranoid delusions associated with smoking weed. So pot heads across the globe, we all should just all relax, take a deep breath and count to ten. That way, you won't turn every minor concern that might cross our minds, into some apocalyptic doomsday scenario. That way you'll continue to think clearly. You don't want to end up like Warren "Peanunt" Robinson. He lost everything because he was always paranoid. Instead of being paranoid at the right time.

THE "OH SHIT, I'M GONNA DIE" SYNDROME

From time to time, after smoking some raw weed, many blunt smokers will suffer a severe panic attack, that we call the "Oh shit, I'm gonna die!" syndrome. The name comes from the phrase, that most often jumps into the mind of the pot head, prior to the panic attack. The symptoms of this panic attack usual are the following, rapid heart beat, dizziness, a feeling of dread or impending death. Best way to combat this, is to drink some thing. And we're not talking about juice or water. A beer or some hard liquor usual calms the nerves and can help even you out. Splashing some cold water into the face several times will also help. Or just lay down and wait for the episode to pass. Its also helpful to try to calm yourself down by telling yourself repeatedly, that you're only suffering a panic attack induced by weed.

SHORT TERM MEMORY

Short term memory is a chronic phenomenon, that sadly effects all pot heads, that smoke weed on a regular basis. The author of this book had compiled extensive notes on the subject, so the reader could have an in-depth understanding of the matter. But unfortunately the author was also smoking a blunt at the time and had all the notes stored up in his head. You know the rest. Short term memory strikes again. Next subject.

STUCK ON STUPID

Short term memory sufferers will also be afflicted with another hideous disease, that goes by the name of "Stuck on Stupid". This condition occurs when your short term memory, coordination, and communications skills all malfunction at the same time. The condition can last anywhere from a couple of seconds, or for several days in some extreme cases. One has a greater chance of being stricken with the disease if you smoke high grade weed, such as Haze or Hydro. The disease is relatively harmless, but it can also become very embarrassing if you catch an attack of stuck on stupid while out on a date.

A bad episode of stuck on stupid happened to one Raymond Lee, while out on a date, with a young lady he was trying to hook up with for years. Raymond had finally gathered up enough courage to ask this particular young lady out on a date. She agreed and they both hooked up on a Saturday night to see a movie at their local Cineplex. Everything was going as planned. Raymond and the young lady were hitting it off well. During their conversation Raymond discovered that his date smoked weed as well. It seemed to be a match made in heaven.

Raymond offered to buy some haze so they could smoke out before the movie started. The young lady agreed. Raymond went and copped a twenty bag of haze, dumping the entire bag of haze into a dutch and lit it up. But after they both smoked the potent haze, things went down hill. Raymond caught a case of stuck on stupid. He couldn't speak anymore because he was at a lost for words. He started to sweat profusely and just made a complete ass of himself. He couldn't escape from the nightmare of being stuck on stupid. After the date was over the young lady wouldn't return Raymond's phone calls anymore. He was heart broken but also learnt a valuable lesson. Being stuck on stupid can definitely hamper your social life when it comes to being with the ladies.

LAZINESS

Smoking weed has many benefits. However, laziness is not one of them. During the writing process of this book, I was tempted to do extensive research on the debilitating topic of laziness. But unfortunately I ran into a session and got stone out of my mind. Making me way too lazy to research the topic any further.

MUNCHIES

This is the most complex, and consistent syndrome out of the entire group. Some times suffering through a bout of the munchies can be a very annoying thing. At other times it can be a blissful experience. But first let us define the word "Munchies". The definition is simple; Weed induced starvation. It takes anywhere between five, to ten minutes after smoking some weed, for the munchies to attack. And there's no deny the urge to eat once this syndrome takes hold of you.When you're dead broke and your pockets are low. Having the munchies can be pure hell. When it comes to buying food or buying some weed. A true pot head will spend his money on weed first and worry about eating later. Starvation on an empty stomach ain't the move. That's the equivalent of smoking weed on a empty stomach.

If all possible one should try to eat a meal prior to smoking some weed. Eating something before lighting up, will slow the onslaught of the munchies by thirty minutes. Occasionally, the munchies can even serve as a festive addition to certain situations. Where pigging out on some food will occur. If there's a cook out, dinner at a restaurant, holiday meal, or anytime you want to enhance your dinning experience. Smoke some weed and once the munchies hit, those meals will become long lasting memories of some of the best food you ever had.

7

FACTS

ECONOMICS

This subject strikes a delicate nerve with many poor and working class pot heads around the world. Any objective person, realizes, they spend way too much money on weed, during a given day, week, or month. There are many equations to figure out ones annual cost on cannabis. Here are just a few of them.

If you buy a nickel bag (and this is rare because five dollar bags of weed are practically extinct), every day then the following equations is for you.

$5 (bag of weed) X 365 (days in a year) = $1,825.

The following equations are the going rate for weed times they days of the week.

$10 X 365 = $3,650.

$20 X 365 = $7,300

$30 X 365 = $10,950

$50 X 365 = $18,250

$100 X 365 = $36,500.

Now some of us smoke more and some of us smoke less. No matter what our daily intake, we spend way too much money on weed. If one saved all the money, they spent on weed, they could have a whip, house, or could spend more money tricking at the strip club.

RECYCLING

If you have been smoking for years then you'll understand the use of roaches. For those of you who don't know, roaches are the small ends of a blunt, or joints, that's not smoked. Often time you'll see them laying around in the ash tray waiting for their call to duty. When a pot head runs out of weed, roaches are the reserve force, that comes in and saves the day. Once you unwrap the roaches, small amounts of weed and residue will come out. One can take these small amounts of weed and create a blunt. Now the weed won't get you high like a fresh bud of weed. But it will get you high enough. So keeping roaches is a great way to save yourself on a rainy day. If you plan ahead, try to out the blunt with half an inch of blunt left. That way when you come back to the roaches, you'll have enough weed saved in the roaches to get high.

THE LAW

Marijuana violators in the United States are arrested at the rate of one every 42 seconds. So that means watch your ass. Now if you have to purchase your weed from a local weed spot, just remember you might be confronted by police officers. That's when you have two options. First option, is to throw away the weed (so it won't be in your possession if the cops arrest you) and take off running as fast as you can. The second option is to give up and hope you won't spend more then a night in jail for possession of weed. In 2003 there were 755,187 people arrested for weed.

8

FREQUENTLY ASKED QUESTIONS

The following material has been painstakingly researched over several months of visiting ivory league colleges, and top notch medical facilities, to get the most accurate information so I could dispel or confirm several marijuana myths.

Well, let me stop lying. I was too high and too lazy, to go through all that trouble. I just surfed the internet and got the following information.

CAN MARIJUANA CAUSE BRAIN DAMAGES?

The most celebrated study that claims to show brain damage is the rhesus monkey study done in the late 70's. Health workers was sharply criticized for its insufficient sample size (only four monkeys), and the misidentification of normal monkey brain structure as "damaged". Actual studies of human populations of marijuana users have shown no evidence of brain damage.

CAN MARIJUANA SUPPRESSE THE IMMUNE SYSTEM?

Like the studies claiming to show damage to the reproductive system, this myth is based on studies where animals were given extremely high, in many cases, near-lethal, doses of cannabinoids. These results have never been duplicated in human beings.

IS MARIJUANA MUCH MORE DANGEROUS THAN TOBACCO?
Smoked marijuana contains about the same amount of carcinogens as does an equivalent amount of tobacco. It should be remembered, however, that a heavy tobacco smoker consumes much more tobacco than a heavy marijuana smoker consumes marijuana. When all of these facts are taken together, it can be clearly seen that the reverse is true: marijuana is much SAFER than tobacco.

Legal marijuana would cause carnage on the highways? Although marijuana, when used to intoxication, does impair performance in a manner similar to alcohol. Actual studies of the effect of marijuana on the automobile accident rate suggest that it poses LESS of a hazard than alcohol. For example, an economic analysis of the effects of decriminalization on marijuana usage found that states that had reduced penalties for marijuana possession experienced a rise in marijuana use and a decline in alcohol use with the result that fatal highway accidents decreased. This would suggest that, far from causing "carnage", legal marijuana might actually SAVE LIVES.

CAN MARIJUANA "FLATTEN" HUMAN BRAINWAVES?

This is an out-and-out lie perpetrated by the Partnership for a Drug-Free America. In reality, marijuana has the effect of slightly increasing alpha wave activity. Alpha waves are associated with meditative and relaxed states which are, in turn, often associated with human creativity.

CAN WEED CAUSE OVERDOSE ??

No fatal overdose due to cannabis use has ever been recorded in humans. Only with intravenous administration, a method rarely or never used by humans, may such a level be possible. Also, some evidence suggests that toxic levels may be higher for humans than for rats.

DOES WEED MAKE WHITE WOMEN CRAZY FOR BLACK MEN?

In the late 30's a 'drug czar' Henri Aslinger charged that the drug (marijuana) provoked murderous behavior in previously solid citizen. Mr. Aslinger also testified that cannabis "makes Darkies feel equal to white men". He told the white men in the audience "Gentlemen, it will make your wives want to have sex with a Black man!"

DID THE GOVERNMENT MAKE ITS OWN STRAIN?

G13 is the alleged code name for a strain of marijuana, supposedly developed by several U.S. Government agencies during the 1960's. According to the myth, the CIA, FBI, and other agencies procured the best strains of more powerfully intoxicating marijuana from breeders all over the world. G13 strain provided a very potent smoke and a completely mellow high. Allegedly a single cutting of this potent strain was stolen by an employee at this government facility and released to the public. The name comes from the room the employee supposedly stole it from. Some dealers claim to sell descendants strains of the G13.

Like they say in the hood. The biggest drug house in America, is the White House. There's no surprise that Uncle Sam was not only selling weed for medical purposes to terminally ill patients. But they were also trying to make the most potent weed possible. Why would the government do this, you might ask? Well whoever has the strongest weed, is gonna make the most sales. And you best believe Uncle Sam wants to have the rawest weed on the block. After all this is a capitalist society.

Is weed Spiritual?

In China hemp was so highly regarded in ancient China that the Chinese called their country "the land of mulberry and hemp". Hemp was a symbol of power over evil. The only way to cure the sick was to drive out the demons. The early doctors used marijuana stalks into which snake-like figures were carved.

In Japan hemp was used in Ancient Japan in ceremonial purification rites and for driving away evil spirits. Clothes made of hemp were especially worn during formal and religious ceremonies because of hemp's traditional association with purity.

When the white man first went to Africa, marijuana was part of everyday life. The Africans were observed inhaling the smoke from piles of smoldering hemp in religious ceremonies. The African Dagga (marijuana) cults believed that Holy Cannabis was brought to earth by the gods. Throughout the ancient world Ethiopia was considered the home of the gods.

The present day Cuna Indians of Panama use marijuana as a sacred herb and the Cora Indians of the Sierra Madre Occidental of Mexico smoke marijuana in this course of their sacred ceremonies.
Moslems considered hemp as a "Holy Plant".
It is interesting to note that the use of hemp was not prohibited by Mohammed (570-632 A.D) while the use of alcohol was. The Sufis (a Moslem sect) originating in 8th century Persia used hashish as a means of stimulating

mystical consciousness and appreciation of the nature of Allah. Eating hashish to the Sufis was "an act of worship". They maintained that hashish gave them otherwise unattainable insights into themselves, deeper understanding and that it made them feel witty. They also claimed that it gave happiness, reduced anxiety, reduced worry, and increased music appreciation.

Looks like blunt smoking has been a part of the spiritual way of life since the dawn of religion. When it comes to hypocrites and weed smokers, it looks like us pot heads go further back with religion. And if you think about it, I'm quite sure, all the blasphemers, hypocrites, and false witnesses, started going to church when religion started letting people join the church that didn't smoke weed.

So the next time you see that stuck up, old woman. That wears that funny hat to church each Sunday looking down at you because you're smoking a blunt just two doors down from the church. Just wink at her. Because by smoking that blunt you're reaching a spiritual level she'll never obtain. But hold up. Don't sleep. Those old church Ladies be lighting up weed too, after services is over on the low. Take my word for it. I know. Because I've smoked out with a few old church Ladies in my time.

9

THE TESTIMONIAL

To give the readers insight into the world of blunt smoking, the author gathered a group of pot heads together to participate in a real life session. Several bags of purple haze and a box of Dutchmaster cigars were provided. The gentlemen present were asked to reflect on their years of rolling and smoking blunts. The gentlemen were the following:

JASON PORTER age 35, employee for the united states postal service. He claims, over the past seven years he's been able to beat random drug tests at his job, by taking Herbal Cleansers which he cops at his local Jamaican weed spot. He's been smoking weed for over twenty years.

DEREK WRIGHT, age 21, young aspiring rapper, right now getting his grind on working in the music industry, doing street team promotions for Def Jam records. One of the perks of working in the music industry is you don't have to worry about random drug tests at the job. In fact you can light up and smoke a blunt in the Def jam offices after 5pm every day.

TONE WITHMORE, age 24, recent college graduate, currently teaching in a New York City public high school. He claims that the most potent dime bag of haze he ever cop was from one of his students in his 10th grade social science class.'

MICHAEL LOPEZ, age 29, works as a real estate broker, he claims that he's closed many of his deals by just lighting up with some of his clients. Since he lives up in the Washington Heights area of New York City he has access to some of the best purple haze and hydro money can buy.

Q. *My first question is let's go back to the beginning. When did you guys start smoking weed?*

JASON PORTER: Well, I think I'm the oldest cat here, I'm not sure but I bet a lot of brothers back in the day don't remember trey bags of weed.

MICHAEL LOPEZ: I remember trey bags.

JASON PORTER: The last place you could go cop a trey bag was up on 127 street and 7th avenue. That was back in the late 80's and early 90's. But back to your original question.

When I started smoking weed I was around 10 years old. I went out with my older cousin Walt, to this movie theater down on 42nd street, that would play three karate flicks for the price of one. Well anyway I was feeling like a big man since I was hanging with my older cousin. When we were in the theater and he started to roll up some weed, I asked could I get a couple of tokes. The rest is history.

DEREK WRIGHT: I started smoking weed after I saw the first Friday movie staring Ice Cube and Chris Tucker. Once I saw the movie it was a wrap. I had to start smoking weed.

MICHAEL LOPEZ: That's funny because my generation and I think Jason can elaborate, we grew up with Cheech & Chong, this generation has the Friday movies to inspire them to smoke weed.

TONE WITHMORE: I'm a late bloomer when it comes to smoking weed. I didn't start smoking regularly until I was in college. I mean I tried off and on during junior high and high school but I became a full time weed head during my college years.

Q. Do you guys think weed is addictive?

DEREK WRIGHT: Hell-fucking-yeah!

MICHAEL LOPEZ: All the money I've spent on weed over the years, I could have bought me a house or some real estate by now.

JASON PORTER: I would have to say weed is probably the most addictive drug there is. Society won't admit it, because quiet as kept, everyone is smoking weed on the down low. Weed is way more widespread then people could ever imagine.

TONE WITHMORE: Well I read all the studies while I was in school. I think I did a paper on drug abuse my first year in college. All the studies say weed isn't addictive, but from personal experience, I would have to say that all those studies were bullshit.

Q. Do you guys consider yourself drug abusers?

TONE WITHMORE: That all depends on how society labels something. For instance if you consider marijuana a drug, then you would have to say yes, I consider myself a drug abuser. But I personally don't see things that way, because I don't consider marijuana a drug. I consider it a plant that possess a chemical by the name of THC, that gives me pleasure. To me drugs are a man made creation. From the last time I heard man hasn't been able to create a weed plant, only nature can do that.

JASON PORTER: I have to agree on that. Drugs like heroin and coke is something that you abuse, weed is just something you enjoy.

DEREK WRIGHT: I might not be a drug abuser but I'm sure as hell a straight up hard core weed abuser.

MICHAEL LOPEZ: Amen to that.

Q. Does rolling weed in Blunts improve your weed experience?

DEREK WRIGHT: Right now this haze we've been smoking got me stuck on stupid so maybe someone else can answer your question.

JASON PORTER: For one, smoking weed in a blunt has several advantages, but at the same time smoking weed in rolling paper has its advantages as well. The number one advantage to smoking weed in a blunt, and when we say blunt we're generalizing all the cigars that one uses to smoke weed in. But the first advantage is that a blunt will burn slower so that helps when you have a lot of heads in a session. Also the tobacco that's in the cigar paper gives you a slight buzz that accompanies the weed high.

MICHAEL LOPEZ: Its funny a lot cats that smoke weed claim they don't smoke cigarettes, but they still inhaling tobacco when they smoke weed in blunts. I wonder how many of us are gonna come down with lung cancer. Because we're still taking in all the same poisons that goes along with cigarettes.

TONE WITHMORE: That's why soon, I'm gonna give up smoking weed in blunts and switch to rolling paper.

JASON PORTER: When I'm dolo smoking by myself I usually roll my weed up in rolling paper. I only smoke blunts when I'm in a session. If I'm dolo and smoking some haze I might roll it up in a dutch, because haze and dro don't burn too well in rolling paper. But I had to stop smoking blunts all the time because I'm getting older and I'm not a young buck anymore like my man Derek over there.

Q. DO YOU THINK PEOPLE WILL STILL BE USING CIGARS TO SMOKE THEIR WEED, IN THE NEXT TEN OR TWENTY YEARS?

JASON PORTER: That's a real good question. Its already been twenty years of people using cigars to smoke their weed in. And common sense would tell you that people probably were using cigars to smoke weed in ever since the two combination have been available. A pot head would use any tool to smoke weed in as long as they can get high. Who knows maybe bongs or pipes will make a come back.

MICHAEL LOPEZ: And remember things like rolling paper, bongs, and pipes, have never went out of style. Its just more popular to smoke weed nowadays in a blunt, then it is in rolling paper.

TONE WITHMORE: And I bet that statistically more people use rolling paper then do blunts. But since all the rappers are promoting blunt use, then that makes it more public, but I bet rolling paper is still the predominate tool used to smoke weed in.

DEREK WRIGHT: Fuck cigars, rolling paper, bongs and pipes, the future of smoking weed won't be smoking at all. Motherfuckers are gonna be popping THC pills. I heard they already have a pattern on the THC pill. That's why they want to keep weed illegal, so the pharmaceutical companies can sell it to the masses. Imagine being able to go to your local drug store and by some Haze pills. That's the future.

TONE WITHMORE: That's funny because I read the same thing. I also heard that the Bush family owns one of the pharmaceutical companies that owns the patent on the THC pills.

MICHAEL LOPEZ: If you want to get real deep lets go all the way back in the days. And you would have to ask yourself, why did they make weed illegal in the first place? Well some people believe its because of Phillip Randolh Hearts. Back in the day, this Hearts motherfucker, was this newspaper publisher, and was like the richest motherfucker on the earth. Now Hearts was also a major player in the timber industry. Now you need timber to publish newspapers but lets not forget hemp can be used to make paper as well.

So some people think Hearts used his newspapers to write articles and editorials to demonized marijuana use. Sure enough around 1938 or 39 they made weed illegal in this country. Once they made weed illegal hemp became an unlikely competitor to the timber industry.

JASON PORTER: Another reason they wanted to make weed illegal, is because they know once brothers like us sit down and spark a session, our mental can raise to such a higher level of consciousness. Our mental powers alone can take over shit in a minute.

Q. Do you guys think people will ever give up smoking weed?

DEREK WRIGHT: Well I'm high until I die. I don't give a fuck if the entire world stops smoking weed, I'll be smoking weed until my lungs can't take it anymore. When that day happens I'll buy those THC pills and keep my grind on.

JASON PORTER: One day I was up in the weed spot and this Rasta pulled me to the side and showed me a passage in the Bible. I think it was in Psalms where it said; When there is Herb around there will be peace among men. So weed has been around since before the bible. And if you ask me weed will never go anywhere. It was probably growing on this Earth before mankind and when mankind leaves this Earth, weed will still be growing on this planet. I guess weed will never disappear.

MICHAEL LOPEZ: Yo, imagine if weed just disappeared from the Earth. Imagine if the plant became extinct? What would happen?

DEREK WRIGHT: Son, I don't even want to think about that.

JASON PORTER: Yeah that would be a fucking nightmare.

MICHAEL LOPEZ: If weed became extinct it would be a fucking riot. People would go crazy not just in this country but around the world. What does that tell you? That weed is part of the fabric of humanity.

10

THE LAST TOKE

Like all good sessions, or a fat dutch full of haze, its time to take the last toke and bring this journey down the subculture of rolling blunts to an end. What have we learnt? Well if you did learn anything, I'm quite sure you forgot it all by now, because of the enormous amount of weed you smoked, during the six months it took you to read this book. And for all you real slow people out there you can wait for our second book, "Rolling Blunts for Dumber, Dummies". That book should help all those that couldn't be helped by this one. In closing, spread the gospel of twisting L's, and dumping haze into blunts. And one day you will be granted the title, master of rolling the dutch.

THE END

11

APPENDIX

It wouldn't be fair, if I didn't continue my illegal literary activities, by teaching you how to grow some chronic. This next essay is on how to produce hydro weed. If you want further information hit up the web site Weed seed shop. com. There's a wealth of information for us blunt heads. And remember, get arrested on your own discretion. This book is for satire purposes only.

HOW TO GROW HYDRO

Most growers report that a hydroponic system will grow weed plants faster than a soil medium, given the same genetics and environmental conditions. This may be due to closer attention and more control of nutrients, and more access to oxygen. The weed plants can breath easier, and therefor, take less time to grow. One report has it that weed plants started in soil matured after hydroponic weed plants started 2 weeks later! Fast growth allows for earlier maturation and shorter total growing time per crop. Also, with soil mixtures, weed plant growth tends to slow when the Weed plants become root-bound. Hydroponics provides even, rapid growth with no pauses for transplant shock and eliminates the labor/ materials of repotting if rockwool is used. (Highly recommended!)

By far the easiest hydroponic systems to use are the wick and reservoir systems. These are referred to as Passive Hydroponic methods, because they require no water distribution system on an active scale (pump, drain, flow meter and path). The basis of these systems is that water will wick to where you want it if the medium and conditions are correct.

The wick system is more involved than the reservoir system, since the wicks must be cut and placed in the pots, correct holes must be cut in the pots, and a spacer must be created to place the weed plants up above the water reservoir below. This can be as simple as two buckets, one fit inside the other, or a kiddie pool with bricks in it that the pots rest on, elevating them out of the nutrient solution.

I find the wick setup to be more work than the reservoir system. Initial setup is a pain with wicks, and the weed plants sit higher in the room, taking up precious vertical space. The base the pot sits on may not be very stable compared to a reservoir system, and a knocked over weed plant will never be the same as an untouched weed plant, due to stress and shock in recovery.

The reservoir system needs only a good medium suited to the task, and a pan to sit a pot in. If rockwool slabs are used, a half slab of 12" rockwool fits perfectly into a kitty litter pan. The roots spread out in very desirable horizontal fashion and have a lot of room to grow. Plants grown in this manner are very robust because they get a great deal of oxygen at the roots. Plants grown with reservoir hydroponics grow at about the same rate as wicks or other active hydroponic methods, with much less effort required, since it is by far the simplest of hydroponic methods. Plants can be watered and feed by merely pouring solution into the reservoir every few days. The pans take up very little vertical space and are easy to handle and move around.

In a traditional hydroponic method, pots are filled with lava/ vermiculite mix of 4 to 1. Dolite Lime is added, one Tblspn. per gallon of growing medium. This medium will wick and store water, but has excellent drainage and air storage capacity as well. It is however, not very resuable, as it is difficult to recapture and sterilize after harvest. Use small size lava, 3/8" pea size, and rinse the dust off it, over and over, until most of it is gone. Wet the vermiculite (dangerous dry, wear a mask) and mix into pots. Square pots hold more than round. Vermiculite will settle to bottom after repeated watering from the top, so only water from the top occasionally to leach any mineral deposits, and put more vermiculite on the top than the bottom. Punch holes in the bottom of the pots, and add water to the pan. It will be wicked up to the roots and the weed plants will have all they need to flourish.

The reservoir is filled with 1

One really great hydroponic medium is Oasis floral foam. Stick lots of holes into it to open it up a little, and start Weed plants/clones in it, moving the cube of foam to rockwool later for larger growth stages. Many prefer floral foam, as it is inert, and adds no PH factors. It's expensive though, and tends to crumble easily. I'm also not sure it's very reusable, but it seems to be a popular item at the indoor gardening centers.

Planting can be made easier with hydroponic mediums that require little setup such as rockwool. Rockwool cubes can be reused several times, and are premade to use for hydroponics. Some advantages of rockwool are that it is impossible to over water and there is no transplanting. Just place the weed plant's cube on top of a larger rockwool cube and enjoy your extra leisure time.

Some find it best to save money by not buying rockwool and spending time weed planting in soil or hydroponic mediums such as vermiculite/lava mix. Pearlite is nice, since it is so light. Pearlite can be used instead of or in addition to lava, which must be rinsed and is much heavier.

But rockwool has many advantages that are not appreciated until you spend hours repotting; take a second look. It is not very expensive, and it is reusable. It's more stable than floral foam, which crunches and powders easily. Rockwool holds 10 times more water than soil, yet is impossible to over-water, because it always retains a high percentage of air. Best of all, there is no transplanting; just place a starter cube into a rockwool grow cube, and when the weed plant gets very large, place that cube on a rockwool slab. Since rockwool is easily reused over and over, the cost is divided by 3 or 4 crops, and ends up costing no more than vermiculite and lava, which is much more difficult to reclaim, sterilize and reuse (repot) when compared to rockwool. Vermiculite is also very dangerous when dry, and ends up getting in the carpet and into the air when you touch it (even wet), since it dries on the fingers and becomes airborne. For this reason, I do not recommend vermiculite indoors.

Rockwool's disadvantages are relatively few. It is alkaline PH, so you must use something in the nutrient solution to make it acidic (5.5) so that it brings the rockwool down from 7.7, to 6.5 (vinagar works great.) And it is irritating to the skin when dry, but is not a problem when wet.

To pre-treat rockwool for weed planting, soak it in a solution of fish emulsion, trace mineral solution and phosphoresic acid (PH Down) for 24 hours, then rinse. This will decrease the need for PH worries later on, as it buffers the rockwool PH to be fairly neutural.

Hydroponics should be used indoors or in greenhouses to speed the growth of weed plants, so you have more bud in less time. Hydroponics allows you to water the weed plants daily, and this will speed growth. The main difference between hydroponics and soil growing is that the hydroponic soil or "medium"is made to hold moisture, but drain well, so that there are no over-watering problems associated with continuous watering. Also, hydroponically grown weed plants do not derive nutrients from soil, but from the solution used to water the weed plants. Hydroponics reduces worries about mineral buildup in soil, and lack of oxygen to suffocating roots, so leaching is usually not necessary with hydroponics.

Hydroponics allows you to use smaller containers for the same given size weed plant, when compared to growing in soil. A feedings, and the medium passes on oxygen much more redily when the roots become bound in the small container. Plant food is administered with most waterings, and allows the gardener to strictly control what nutrients are available to the weed plants at the different stages of Weed plant growth. Watering can be automated to some degree with simple and cheap drip system apparatus, so take advantage of this when possible. Hydroponics will hasten growing time, so it takes less time to harvest after weed planting. It makes sense to use simple passive hydroponic techniques when possible. Hydroponics may not be desirable if your growing outdoors, unless you have a greenhouse.

CAUTION: it is necessary keep close watch of weed plants to be sure they are never allowed to dry too much when growing hydroponically, or roots will be damaged. If you will not be able to tend to the garden every day, be sure the pans are filled enough to last until next time you return, or you can easily lose your crop.

More traditional hydroponic methods (active) are not discussed here. I don't see any point in making it more diffucult than it needs to be. It is necessary to change the solution every month if your circulating it with a pump, but the reservoir system does away with this problem. Just rinse the medium once a month or so to prevent salts build up by watering from the top of the pot or rockwool cube with pure water. Change weed plant foods often to avoid deficiencies in the weed plants. I recommend using 2 different Weed plant foods for each phase of growth, or 4 foods total, to lessen chances of any type of deficiency.

Change the solution more often if you notice the PH is going down quickly (too acid). Due to cationic exchange, solution will tend to get too acid over time, and this will cause nutrients to become unavailable to the weed plants. Check PH of the medium every time you water to be sure no PH issues are occuring.

Algae will tend to grow on the medium with higher humidities in hydroponics. It will turn a slab of rockwool dark green. To prevent this, use the plastic cover the rockwool came in to cover rockwool slab tops, with holes cut for the weed plants to stick out of it. It's easy to cut a packaged slab of rockwool into two pieces, then cut the end of the plastic off each piece. You now have two pieces of slab, each covered with plastic except on the very ends. Now cut 2 or 3 4" square holes in the top to place cubes on it, and place each piece in a clean litter pan. Now your ready to treat the rockwool as described above in anticipation of Weed planting. If growing in pots, a layer of gravel at the top of a pot may help reduce algae growth, since it will dry very quickly. Algae is merely messy and unsightly; it will not actually cause any complications with the weed plants.